I0670827

Almost Christmas

Nathan Graziano

Redneck Press Revere MA

Book design by d'Entremont
Cover photo from the collection of Lauren Leja

ISBN-13: 978-0692986479

Redneck Press
119 Bradstreet Avenue
Revere MA 02151
redneckpress@gmail.com
www.friedchickenandcoffee.com/manifesto/the-
chapbooks/

To Mikey

Acknowledgments

Some of these pieces originally appeared, in different forms, in the following journals: *The Coe Review, Drunk Monkeys, Fiction 365, Flash Fiction Magazine, The Fox Cry Review, Freight Stories, Fried Chicken and Coffee, Full of Crow, Night Train, Red Fez, Storyglossia, The Meadow, The Trailer Park Quarterly* and *Wilderness House Literary Review.*

"You said, "'You're killing yourself.'"
I said, "I know, but if I don't no one else will.
It's a hell of a way to go,
Painless and slow,
There's always time to kill.'"

—Dan Cray, *More than Booze*

Contents

Santa, Baby

My Favorite Things

I'll Be Home

Santa, Baby

The Proud Father

His bottom lip quivers as he rises before the judge, the jury, and the television cameras. He is your son, your only child, and he recently turned eighteen. In his new navy-blue suit and tie—the navy-blue suit and tie you bought him with the money you and your wife had saved for his first semester books at Dartmouth College—he reminds you of his six-year-old self, a boy with a high blush and a hairless face.

As you watch him, your chest tightens, your left arm goes numb, and you wonder if forty-six is too young to have a heart attack. Your son is being tried as an adult, and you wish you could trade places with his attorney, the man you can't afford, the man with a wizened white beard and a hand resting on your son's shoulder. You want to be close to your son, to hold him.

Your wife squeezes your hand and whimpers. You want to hold her as well, despite her threats of divorce and the accusations that it was you who failed to raise him to be a decent man. She used that word: *decent*.

You glance across the aisle at the alleged victim and her family, her father hugging her as she wipes her eyes and waits. You want to believe that she perjured herself. You want to believe she is trying to save face for a bad decision she made after she left the party that night, drunk, with your son. You want to believe that she consented, and your son — in a terrible moment of unchecked passion — bit the girl's breast then apologized, like he testified. You want to believe that you're all decent people, parents and children alike, and that something occurred that night in a bedroom behind a locked door, something as ambiguous as a Rorschach test. It was something utterly unknowable, something mired in reasonable doubt.

And now, as the jury stands in front of your son, and your wife's hand is sweating and her breathing is labored, you watch him, your boy. He's the boy you coached in Little League, the second baseman and lead-off hitter on a last-place team; the boy you taught to whistle through an acorn; the boy you taught to jump-start a stick shift by pushing it down a hill and punching the clutch; the boy you taught to tie a Windsor Knot, something your father taught you. This is your son, and you know, beneath the banter and the bravado, there is a sensitive kid; someone you've been proud to call your son for eighteen years—an honor roll student and an average athlete, a boy who writes poetry but is too insecure to share it with anyone other than you and your wife and, allegedly, the girl across the aisle. And you know—and this is what startles you from sleep—he won't fare well in prison, being so young and fresh-faced and hardly needing to shave.

You wonder, as you squeeze your wife's hand and ignore the tightening in your chest, if your son did what the girl said, if the events happened the way the girl, talking through choked sobs, testified. You wonder if your son—and this terrifies you most—is capable of being so monstrous. Then you question yourself and your own decency.

"Has the jury reached a decision?" The judge asks, peering over her bifocals.

"We have, Your Honor."

The bailiff takes the slip of paper from the head juror and hands it to the judge, who reads it, stone-faced, and hands it back. Your wife whimpers. Your son squeezes his eyes shut and bites on his bottom lip to keep it from quivering. For a second, the courtroom is as airless as a catacomb. The head juror clears his throat. The cameras click, all of them pointed at your son.

Your heart beats with your son's heart, and you are back to a Christmas morning, your son smiling, silver wrapping paper wadded around him. Later, as he played his new video game, giggling, your wife asked if you wanted to try for another. You made love that night. But after the tests and procedures, the false hopes and expensive attempts at in vitro, you eventually accepted that you were happy to have one—the proud father of a son.

As the head juror reads the decision, your son's head drops like the tendons were cut from his neck. When he turns to you and wails, and your wife wails, too, your legs give and your chest tightens.

Nathan Graziano

Opening Day

The forecast is calling for rain on Opening Day. Not showers but a Biblical downpour. The husband is packing his books, his horror novels and his James Patterson collection, into boxes he grabbed from the liquor store. The wife stands in the doorway of their bedroom, her arms crossed. "Will you be out the house by Thursday?"

"I'm going to Fenway on Thursday," the husband says. "It's Opening Day." He reaches onto the next shelf for the Dean Koontz books and the biology textbook from that one year at community college. "I'll be out by the weekend."

"Is your girlfriend going to help you move?" The wife says "girlfriend" like she's spitting poison, like there is something toxic in the syllables.

"She's not my girlfriend," he says. "It didn't mean anything."

"I hate you."

"I know." He takes a box cutter from the pocket of his jeans. If this were a horror story, he'd slice off a small piece of scalp—nothing life threatening, only a piece of skin the size of a dime.

With her back turned, the wife says, "Why can't you be out by Thursday? I can't stand looking at you."

"Thursday is Opening Day. I'm going to Fenway."

"Your son has his first baseball practice on Thursday," the wife says. "You told him you'd take him to his first practice."

"It's supposed to rain." The husband imagines the crack of a bat, the slap of a fastball hitting the catcher's mitt, the static hum of the crowd. He imagines his girlfriend's hand in his, her lips moist with draft beer as they watch the game, waiting for the rain. Everyone is waiting, waiting for something to happen.

The Future Perfect

Emily's breasts are swollen and tender, although the recent emergence of her baby bump is still imperceptible in clothing. But she forgets the discomfort of her breasts as she walks into the foyer of the empty colonial on Kerry Lane and grabs Lucas' hand. She mouths: *This is beautiful.*

Alex — their real estate agent, tall and square-shouldered in a tailored suit with wing-tipped leather shoes — winks at Emily when her husband isn't looking. "At this listing price," Alex says, "I can't imagine it will be on the market long."

Emily glares at Alex as she passes through the foyer and into the kitchen. The black marble counters sparkle, and the stainless steel appliances glitter in the mid-afternoon sunlight. As she runs her fingernails over the countertops, she envisions her Future-self standing in this kitchen, five years from now, on Christmas morning. She will have baked homemade cinnamon rolls, after waking alone at four a.m. to put them in the oven. The Future-Lucas will be sitting at their kitchen table, sipping coffee, as their Future-kids, two blonde boys, play with their toys in the living room.

Then Emily remembers.

"I'm going to check out the basement," says Present-tense Lucas, a licensed home inspector who knows about the guts of houses. "I want to look at the furnace."

"It's brand new," Alex says. Present-tense Lucas' footsteps disappear down the stairs, and Alex approaches Emily from behind, placing his hands on her hips and sliding them up her sides until he is holding her tender breasts.

"Don't," Emily says.

He kisses her neck, his trimmed beard scratching her cheek, his breath hot on her skin. "Let's lock him in the basement."

"Don't," she says as Alex's hard-on presses against her.

"Why?"

"Because I said no."

Alex backs away with his hands raised, a man surrendering. "Then tell him," he says. "Tell him the truth."

"You tell him." Emily notices her reflection in

the microwave door, her face swollen, a tall man standing behind her with his arms folded across his chest.

"Is that what you want?" Alex asks. "Do you want me to tell him the truth? Do you want him to know the truth? You don't think I'll do it?"

"You don't have the balls."

The basement door opens, and Lucas returns in the present tense. While short—slightly under five-five—Emily admires her husband's slim frame and square jaw, the effortless way he wears work boots and blue jeans, the way his hands always feel like a workman's hands. "How many bedrooms are upstairs?" Lucas asks Alex.

"Three," Alex says.

"Perfect," Lucas says to Emily. "This is exactly what we're looking for."

"Alex has something he wants to tell you," she says and takes a deep breath, waiting for Alex to respond.

Alex scratches his beard, whistling a low note but not moving. Then he says, "Maybe it's better if you hear this from your wife."

Emily reaches for her husband's hand but he pulls it away. "We can't buy this house," she says.

Lucas grins without humor. "But this is everything you want, Emily."

She places her hand on her tender breast and

notices her husband's jaw clenching, his Future-fury rising, her Future-self turning into a mist — a mist, and then nothing as the men exchange words.

Nathan Graziano

Birthday at the Hibachi Bar

The hibachi chef balances a green pepper slice on the end of his spatula. There's a metallic clank as he claps his chopping knife against the spatula. The pepper arcs in the air and lands softly into Stephanie's open mouth. The chef, stone-faced, bows to Stephanie.

"That's amazing," Stephanie says, grabbing my arm. "I wish I could do something amazing."

"I heard that they bring some of these chefs from Japan, and they work on visas. Most of them work a year, take in the experience, and return home." I fill our small ceramic cups with warm rice sake. In the dim lighting, no one could guess that Stephanie and I are two decades apart in age. Last semester, she was one of my composition students at the community college, a fact that shamed me when we first started dating.

Two months ago, the day after my divorce was finalized, I saw Stephanie at a bar where I was drowning my sorrows, doing my whole young-Tom Waits thing, and Stephanie and I started talking. Then we started flirting. Then we started touching. Then we went back to my small apartment, and our clothes came off. I hadn't slept with a woman in almost two years, and being with Stephanie was a small slice of heaven.

We've been dating since that night, seeing each other almost every day. In the past two weeks, we've started going out in public, once at a bookstore and once at a restaurant where the waitress assumed I was her father. We blushed and tried to laugh it off.

Tomorrow, I turn forty-two and I will spend the day with my sixteen year-old son, who is closer to Stephanie's age than mine — they listen to the same music and watch the same shows on Netflix.

My ex-wife says Stephanie is part of my midlife crisis, but I disagree. While Stephanie and I have had more sex in the past month than I had in the last twelve years of my marriage, it is more than the sex. I like her. I like the way she laughs, covering her mouth; I like the way she wants to hold my hand, our fingers entwined, a small intimacy. I like the way she listens when I speak, and I like to hear her speak. Although I'm still unsure what a girl so young and pretty would see in me, a community college professor who can barely afford to live, a middle-aged divorced guy with an adolescent son and a thickening mid-section, we seem to be enjoying each other. And I like it. I like her.

Stephanie slams back the sake then faces me and takes a deep breath. "There's something I need to tell you, Jake." She stares at her fingernails, long and lacquered red.

"Here it comes."

"I'm not breaking up with you," Stephanie says and tucks a strand of brown hair behind her ear. "But I need to tell you something."

Relieved, I run my fingertips across her forearm. "Is it bad?"

"It's not good," she says.

The hibachi chef scoops the rice onto the flattop grill and mixes the vegetables, the stir fry sizzling as he clanks out a steady, martial beat with the spatulas.

"I can almost guarantee you will not surprise me," I tell Stephanie.

"I did a porno," she says in one unpunctuated breath.

I turn my ear toward her mouth. "Excuse me?"

"I did a porno."

"You're a porn star?"

"Not exactly," she says, touching her nail to her lips. "I answered an ad Craig's List to do some modeling. The guy who placed it—some guy living in Merrimack—said I would only have to pose nude and that the picture was for a private collection. He said no one would ever see it and offered me a lot of money. I was nineteen, living on my own. He then offered me more money for other things. I mean, it paid my rent for the rest of the year."

I shake my head as the spatula's backbeat quickens.

"I was doing a lot of coke at the time," she says.

"Can I watch it?"

Her eyes are wide then gloss over. We wait for the first tear to run down her cheek and drop onto her lap. "I thought you respected me," she says.

"I do," I say and suddenly I have this horrific image of my sixteen year-old son watching a clip of my girlfriend fucking a disembodied man behind a camera, a man whose face never appears.

The hibachi chef holds up a plastic squirt gun. "Sake, birthday boy."

I open my mouth and he fills it with lukewarm rice wine. Ashamed, I turn to Stephanie and try to shrug and laugh, but she will no longer look at me. It's too late.

Nathan Graziano

Boulder City

They stood in a parking lot outside a roadhouse restaurant, one of a thousand windowless haunts outside The Strip. With his arms around her small waist and her arms wrapping his neck, she rested her head on his chest as the floodlights pressed a singular shadow against the cool pavement. He pulled back.

"Why are you crying?" he asked.

"Because I'm never going to see you again."

"That's not true. I'll call. I'll write. I'll visit. Stop saying that." He glanced at the time on his phone. He knew she would be waiting up, sitting cross-legged on the floor in his empty apartment with a large bottle of Pinot Noir and an ashtray on the rug in front of her.

She kissed him again, longer, framing his face with her hands. "I'm never going to see you again."

"Then I'll stay."

"How can you stay? Your stuff is packed in a truck. And what about her? And what about him?"

"We'll make it work."

"You're just saying that because you're drunk."

"I'm not just saying that," he said. The shadow broke into two pieces, their heads almost touching the moon. A fat man with a handlebar mustache, carrying a carton of leftovers, staggered past them, weaving through the cars. He waved, and they waved back.

"Let's get a room in Boulder City," he said. "Like we did that night."

She laughed. "If the Justice of the Peace had answered his phone."

"I would've done it."

"Me too," she said. "Now I'm never going to see you again."

"Then I'm staying here. With you."

"Now I know you're drunk."

"I am drunk. And I'm staying here with you." He took her small hand in his, held it, and mimed placing a ring on her finger. He kissed her cheek.

"I need to go home," she said. "He thinks I'm out with my friends."

"You are."

When he realized she was leaving, really

leaving, he reached for her hand again but she had left. He found his keys and got into his car as the Las Vegas moon was muted by the lights, all of those lights. Tomorrow, he was moving to the East Coast with a woman he hardly knew. He drove to a convenience store and played video poker for another hour while sobering up. He won twenty bucks.

Rain

When she kicks off a red heel and runs her foot up the hem of your jeans, you whisper that you know a place. "It's called The Kozy 7," you say, "but it's a little seedy."

"It sounds perfect," she says as the lights dim and a cover band of forty-something ex-rockers start their second set by playing the piano solo to "Home Sweet Home" in the wrong key.

You pull into the parking lot, and there's a stretch of dilapidated motel rooms with chipped white paint and weak wooden awnings that an asthmatic breath could blow down. You can tell by her sigh that she didn't anticipate this type of seedy. A red "Vacancy" sign blinks in the window of the main office, and you cut the engine in your old sedan, realizing you're drunker than you thought when you left the bar. You fondle your wedding ring then check your wallet, stunned by your stupidity. "I don't have enough cash," you tell her. "And I can't use my card. My wife checks our bank account every morning."

"So does my husband." She reaches into her purse and produces three twenties. "Will this be enough?"

You nod and take the cash and kiss her on the nose. "I have some Jameson in the trunk."

"Do they have ice?"

"I'll check."

As you walk into the front office, there's a small dog—a Pomeranian, maybe—yipping at you. An old Vietnamese woman behind the front desk shushes him. Everything is tawdry, from the heavy red curtains covering the picture window to the black velvet painting of a hyacinth bush on the wall beside a digital clock that reads 11:12. And while you hand the clerk the cash and your driver's license, proof of who you are—a father of two teenage sons, a husband to a woman who hasn't slept with you in six months and vacillates between counseling and a divorce—you realize you're about to sleep with someone you hardly know, a colleague at the college where you teach, a woman as sad and frustrated and lonely as yourself. In the lobby of the main office, you quietly consent to this.

Back in the car, a key on a green plastic keychain with the number 14 dangles like an ugly Christmas ornament from your index finger, and you notice her head hung, her eyes focused on her phone.

You say, "I know it's not the Hilton—"

"Where are you telling your wife that you're staying tonight?"

"I don't know. Where are you telling your husband?"

"I don't know."

The motel room reeks of stale cigarettes, bleached sheets and Febreze; a framed print of seashells hangs above the bed, dull and deaf. The mattress is high and covered in a stiff quilt with a gaudy floral design. A microwave sits atop a brown mini-fridge, and a flat screen television is mounted on the wall across from the bed. You sit on the edge of the mattress with the whiskey bottle between your legs.

"Is something wrong?" she asks, sitting beside you, kissing your cheek, reaching for the bottle.

You turn and kiss her mouth, her neck, the naked space below her neckline. She kneads your scalp and fakes a moan, such an actress. You place the bottle on the nightstand, shut off the light and, quick, you both slip out of your clothes. Now you're naked beneath the bleached sheets and the stiff quilt, in the dark.

Nathan Graziano

"Are you, you know, fixed?" she asks. "Or do we need a condom?"

"I'm fixed," you say and remember the day you spent on the couch watching the Red Sox game with a bag of frozen peas and a bottle of Vicodin, six months after your second son, Christopher, was born.

There's not much in the name of foreplay — some fumbling of hands seeking assurance, mouths seeking mouths, tongues seeking tongues. Then her tear drops on your nose, and your tear drops down the side of your face. They drop, and they drop.

My Favorite Things

Beans

I was splitting a pitcher with Toby around noon last Monday when he started telling me about this girl he's been seeing who calls painkillers "beans." He said this girl, who is half our age, smokes the pills off foil, inhaling the smoke through a pen tube. Toby said he scores the beans for this girl from someone at the bar.

This girl, Erin, is twenty years old, Toby told me. He said that the merchandise feels new. "I don't think you know her," Toby said.

"I know her," I said. "She used to work here as a waitress."

"You're right."

"She's cute."

Toby nodded and told me that the other night this girl Erin called and asked if he could score her a bean. Toby told me she lived with her grandparents in the old house around the corner across the elementary school that my twin sons attend, not far from my apartment on Taylor Street. Six months ago, I worked at the Hyundai dealership and lived in a house with my wife and sons. Now I'm unemployed and live in an apartment on Taylor Street with no one. My own human noises—the sighs and grunts and whimpers—have started to annoy me.

But this is Toby's story, and Toby told this girl Erin that he could score her a bean and she didn't have to pay for it as long as she had a mouth. She laughed and told him she had a tongue, too.

"That's pretty hot," I said to Toby.

"I fell in love," Toby said.

Toby told me he scored her a Perc 30 from this guy at the bar—he won't tell me who it is—so this girl Erin went to Toby's apartment to smoke the bean with him. Toby told me as soon as she closed the door she dropped to her knees and reached for his belt.

"I need a twenty year-old girl," I said to Toby. "Hell, I just need a girl."

"That's not the whole story," Toby said.

Toby then told me that this girl Erin stopped, held a finger to her lips, and then walked into the other room. Toby zipped his pants and grabbed a beer from the fridge and sat down to watch the Celtics' game.

Ten minutes later, this girl Erin came storming back into the living room and spiked her phone on the couch, sitting beside Toby. Toby told me her cheeks were streaked black where her mascara bled. "It looked like war paint," he told me.

So this girl Erin looks at Toby, rubbing her eyes, and said, "I just broke up with my boyfriend. He called me 'a dumb bitch.' He's so disrespectful."

"You dumped him for being disrespectful to you?" Toby asked this girl, Erin.

So she told him the whole story. She said that earlier that day her boyfriend told her that he smelled cigarettes on her clothes, and this girl Erin had told him that she quit smoking two months ago. The boyfriend is one of those Straight Edge-types so they started arguing and he called her a "dumb bitch."

"But you smoke," Toby said to this girl, Erin.

"I know," she said, "but that was still disrespectful."

So Toby asked her how long they had been dating, and this girl Erin told Toby that she had been dating this guy for two years. Then Toby took a bean from his pocket and placed it in the palm of her hand like a diamond ring.

"Then I smoked it with her," Toby said as the bartender brought us a pitcher. "It's a nice buzz, smoking that shit."

As I was handing the bartender a ten-spot for the pitcher, this girl Erin sent Toby a text. Toby asked me if I wanted to meet this girl, Erin, and one of her friends at the Applebee's in Hooksett at three p.m. "We can go back to my place after and smoke a bean. I have two left."

I looked at Toby then at my beer then at my naked ring finger where I had worn a wedding band for over a decade. I knew what I was going to do. My hair was dusted gray, and I'd gained weight. I was tired of sending out resumes.

Sometimes we all need a bean.

The Incident with the
Chicken Tender

The ladies' bowling team howled when a jowl-faced woman with a flat-top told them a joke about a snail. They had pushed together three tables at the back of the bar and were splitting multiple pitchers of beer. Toby, on the barstool next to me, was staring at his phone and shaking his head. "No beans," he said.

I looked into my beer as if something was lost in it and hiding at the bottom of the glass. "I was looking forward to a bean."

"The Dealer said he has some of the dirty brown."

"Brown?"

"H," he said, his thumbs pounding a text message to the Dealer.

"I don't do needles."

"You don't have to use a needle," Toby said, his eyes fixed on the phone. "We can smoke it like a bean or snort it."

"But it's fucking heroin."

"It's the same thing as a bean. An opiate is an opiate. If you're booting it into your arm, it's a different story. It's next level."

"And if you smoke or sniff it?"

"Same as a bean," he said and picked up his beer. The sky outside the bar was iron-gray, the clouds hanging low, threatening snow. The red and green Christmas lights behind the bar burned in the dimming daylight. "You in?"

I opened my wallet and looked at the forty bucks I had saved for the bean; it was forty bucks I didn't have. "I won't overdose and die, right?"

Toby took my cash. "I can't promise anything."

I sipped my beer as a middle-aged woman from the bowling team, a woman with square shoulders and large hands started to choke on a chicken finger. I stood up as if I were going to do something and play the hero, as if I were going to dislodge the chicken finger from her windpipe myself. Instead I stood still, the consummate coward, waiting to see what would happen next.

The woman in the chair next to the choking person took charge. With calm precision, this woman in a blue track suit performed the Heimlich maneuver. A thumbnail-sized wad of chewed-up chicken finger shot from the choking woman's throat and landed on the dull gray carpet by my feet.

The choking woman coughed and coughed, her knees buckling as she dropped to the floor. I nodded to Toby. At that moment, I knew that half-chewed chicken tender on the dull gray carpet better than I knew myself.

Mudslides

I had been sleeping on Toby's couch for almost a month. I couldn't afford my own place anymore so I started crashing at Toby's and threw him some cash from my unemployment check and the paltry 401K I'd cashed out. The couch was beside a pellet stove that pumped raw, dry heat. On table beside me, there was a tiny ceramic Christmas tree that plugged into the wall. Sometimes, it made me happy but, mostly, it made me miss my family.

I woke that morning dripping sweat but shivering like I was coming down with the flu. It had gotten to the point where sickness stalked me, a sinister shadow, and my days revolved around making it go away.

I looked out the living room window as the sun beat on the snow outside. I didn't like the looks of anything I saw so I pulled a navy-blue fleece blanket over my head, hiding from everything. From the couch, I could smell coffee brewing, and in the kitchen Toby and Tom were talking in low voices. One of them was cleaning dishes, the silverware clanking in the sink.

"I can't keep fronting you," Toby said.

"What are you talking about? I bought shit the other night." Tom was nineteen and already an H-bomb. I suppose the fact that he was nineteen is a significant detail, but I'm not sure why. Maybe it's because Toby and I are older, much older — I'm pushing forty and Toby hopped that fence years ago. Maybe it's because we see ourselves as too old to be junkies. Like mudslides, we already demolished the terrain around us; we have fucked up our lives and the lives of the people close to us, and now there's nothing left. But Tom is young, and somehow that matters.

"You bought that shit three weeks ago, Tom," Toby said. "I can't keep fronting you. I barely have enough cash to support my own habit."

"Fuck this," Tom said. "I'm going to get money."

Toby said, "What are you going to do? Rob a bank?"

"Fuck this." The door to Toby's apartment flew open then slammed shut, and Tom was gone.

Toby's cat Clancy climbed on the couch and sat on my chest. Sweaty and cold and unsettled, I pulled off the blanket and scratched Clancy's head. Toby came into the living room, and Clancy scattered. "Tell me you have some shit," I said.

"That fucking kid," Toby said, taking a framed picture of loons on a lake off the wall. He reached into his pocket and pulled out what looked to be a point-four, but scales are funky and The Dealer often fucks us. Every junkie knows that you can't trust a junkie and the dealer is a junkie. "Let's get filthy," Toby said and started cutting a couple of lines.

I sat up and rubbed my eyes. "There's hope for Tom."

"There's no hope," Toby said and ripped one up his left nostril.

Tom returned an hour later, or four hours later, or three minutes later, holding a Burger King bag with a piece of cardboard tucked under his arm. His cheeks were wine-red, and he was grinning. "I got cash," he said.

Toby and I were sitting on the couch, watching the Patriots' game, a few feet above our bodies. Outside, the sky was dark gray, or maybe it was night.

"Did you rob a bank?" Toby asked, his voice the echo of an old man's voice.

"I stood in front of the shopping plaza holding this sign." Tom held up the piece of cardboard. On the backside of a broken down beer-box, in thick black marker, he wrote, Homeless, anything will help.

A pang of conscience, an acquaintance, awoke. "What the fuck, Tom? That's some real scumbag shit."

Tom shrugged in his bony shoulders. "I made fifty-two bucks, got a pair of gloves and a Whopper-value meal. I would've had more, but this cop showed up and threatened to arrest me."

"People actually gave you money?" Toby asked.

"It's Christmas, man," Tom said and then I remembered it was. Tom looked at me and slapped his forehead. "Nick, I saw your ex-wife in a car with Danny Kostas, and your sons were in the back. Danny gave me ten bucks."

Without the heroin streaming through me, I might have started thinking about the twins, two years before, when they woke up on Christmas morning, squealing at the gifts we had bought them at The Dollar Store and placed beneath the tree; without the heroin streaming through me, I might have cried, or coveted my old life and my ex-wife and everything that fell through a chute with one swift swoosh; without the heroin streaming through me, I might have felt like a junkie, a mudslide.

"Never get married," I said to Tom.

Tom may have heard me but likely he didn't. "Let's get some shit," he said.

"Let's get filthy," I said.

Pick Up

I pick up at a duplex on Somerville Street, fifty yards from the convenience store that has started closing at twilight. At the duplex, a Rottweiler growls in the window as I get out of my car, my head swiveling, looking for cops in unmarked cruisers.

I pick up from the Dealer's Girl. The Dealer found temporary work framing houses so he's not around during the day. Toby, Tom and I all agree that this is a good thing. The Dealer's Girl—a kind but broken woman who speaks in a soft voice and avoids eye contact—sells fatter folds and doesn't cut The China White with sugar to make it weigh. You never know what you're going to get with the Dealer but the Dealer's Girl is fair and consistent, and if she touches your arm, you'll believe in ghosts.

I pick up while the twins are still at school, twenty minutes before I'm supposed to pick them up at the schoolyard.

I pick up inside the duplex where the window to the foyer is covered with a red towel, stifling the sunlight and separating the foyer from a world where there are people who aren't copping, people who buy milk and help their kids with their homework and buy flowers for the people they love. It's a world where people laugh, sometimes.

I pick up then park across from the schoolyard where the twins are waiting for me. I snort a line on the console in my car then stare at the chain-linked fence that separates my children from a world where guys like me draw our daily breaths.

Nathan Graziano

The Androgynous Coat

I finished my beer and grabbed my car keys. "Let's go to the bar," I called to Toby, who was either in his bedroom or someplace far away.

"Come in here," he yelled.

When I walked into the bedroom, Toby had cut two thick lines of dope on his dresser. He handed me a tube and I went for it.

"Look at this," Toby said and held up a red and black-checkered flannel coat. "I picked it up at a yard sale," he said, taking the tube and snorting the second line. "What do you think?"

"Are you sure that's not a woman's coat?"

"I'm not sure," he said and put on the coat and raised his arms. A former bodybuilder, most clothing fits snug around his shoulders, but this looked different, tighter. "Look at the pockets on this thing," Toby said. "There are pockets under the sleeves. There are four pockets on the front, and three pockets inside."

"That's a lot of pockets."

"That's a shitload of pockets," he said. "The other night, I put it on when Erin was here, and she thought it looked like a woman's coat. But the old woman who sold it to me said it belonged to her dead husband."

"Why would either woman lie to you?" I asked. Erin left a pair of black panties on Toby's bedroom floor, and I picked them up and used them to clean my glasses. I fell back into the bed and knew I was about to lift off.

"Why would they make a coat that fits me if it's made for a woman? This doesn't make sense. What type of woman has these shoulders?"

"A wide-shouldered woman," I said. The dope massaged my temples with its feathery hands, and I closed my eyes and floated on the surface of something lazy and fluid. My cell phone buzzed in the front pocket of my jeans, a million tiny pins vibrating down my leg.

"I'm wearing the coat to the bar," Toby said. "You ready?"

Melted into the mattress, I nodded. While in no condition to drive, I reached for my keys and couldn't find them.

An hour later, Toby and I sat on the stools at the

far end of the bar, beside the trivia machine. Toby kept the coat on, every now and then slipping his hand in a new pocket. I started to nod when Toby punched my arm. "Oh shit, Nick."

At the entrance to the bar, my ex-wife stood with Danny Kostas, the bar owner's younger brother. He spotted Toby and me right away and whispered something into my ex-wife's ear. My ex-wife had on a blue and black checkered flannel coat, Toby's coat. She and I looked at each other. Her eyes were ice cold.

When I turned to Toby, he was taking off the coat.

Dirty Little Clouds

Toby smoked the last of our shit and said, "If we buy a gram, Erin and Andrea are willing to barter."

"They're going to fuck us for dope?" I had lifted off and was sitting on the couch, waiting for something to happen. I stared out the living room window, amazed by my ability to forget things. The wind and the freezing rain picked up and pummeled a plastic snowman that the neighbors never put away after Christmas. It was February, I think.

"They're bringing a kit," Toby said and fell back into a couch cushion.

While I hadn't tried shooting, and I'm still not wild about needles, shooting dope seemed like a logical next step. My ex-wife had recently filed papers to prevent me from seeing the twins.

She and Danny Kostas were engaged, and I had arrived at a dangerous place where apathy performed amputations.

I shrugged, listening to the rain with my eyes closed. "How old is her friend?"

"Twenty-one. Same age as Erin," he said. When my ex-wife had moved in with Danny Kostas, she told him about Toby and me, which landed us 86'd from his brother's bar, where we'd spent a good portion of our lives fucking up. I was still homeless and crashing at Toby's place, and my unemployment checks were about to run out.

"So they're giving us sex, and we're paying them with dope? How is this different from prostitution?"

"Quit being such a fucking philosopher," Toby said.

"So do we have to grab, or is the Dealer coming here?"

"The Dealer was here," Toby said and paused. "It's in the top drawer of my dresser."

Although I couldn't see into Toby's bedroom, I knew the top drawer in Toby's scratched wooden dresser was radiating heat. I wiped sweat from the back of my neck and sat up straight on the couch. "You have it in your bedroom?"

"I promised Erin."

Smoke emerged from the bedroom in dirty little

clouds. "We could have a taste, right? To make sure it's good."

Toby walked into the kitchen and returned with a small sheet of foil. "Just a taste," he said. "To make sure."

I fell back on Toby's bed and lifted off onto a dirty little cloud. As I stared at the bedroom ceiling, my ex-wife straddled Danny Kostas on a dirty little cloud beside me, and the twins played a board game on their own dirty little cloud. Toby sat up on the edge of the bed and poured more dope onto a strip of foil.

Someone knocked at the door, followed by the unmistakable but muted sound of young women giggling. Toby had his eyes closed. "We're not here," he said to Clancy, the cat who wasn't in the room.

The knocking continued, and we waited on our dirty little clouds, floating in space, satisfied with our sadness, smoking shit off foil.

The Seagull

It's Tuesday afternoon, and it's raining, a downpour that has left a murky pond in the restaurant's parking lot. Toby and I are splitting pitchers and trying to score a gram, texting various dealers. Fox News is muted on the television behind the bar, a silence that seems to fit as the ticker on the bottom of the screen scrolls the headlines.

A short man walks in, dripping wet. He's lithe and bald with badly dyed black hair pulled into a tight, inky ponytail. He sits beside Toby and orders a Captain and Coke from Cindy, the bartender. The man stares straight into the mirror behind the bar, scowling at his own reflection.

Toby jabs an elbow into my ribs and points at the guy. "Caw, caw, caw!" Toby calls like a bird.

Startled, the man snaps his head to the side

and stares at Toby, a hard stare, unblinking, and as soon as Cindy fixes his Captain and Coke, he snags the drink and moves to a table at the back of the bar, beneath a Budweiser sign.

"Caw, caw, caw," Toby calls again.

"What's that all about?" I ask, waiting for a text.

"That's Jimmy Lucas," Toby says. "I worked with him at The Union Leader about ten years ago. He had more hair then and this weird obsession with Steven Seagal. The guy walked around the warehouse like he was on the set of Hard to Kill, acting all tough with his ponytail and his black hair, kicking his leg in the air and striking karate poses."

I get a text from The Dealer but he is in Lawrence, picking up, and he won't be back for two hours. "What's with the bird call?" I ask.

"Jimmy got a vanity plate and he wanted it to read SEAGAL. But the fucker can't spell so the license plate ended up spelling SEAGUL. So when he'd come into work, we'd make bird calls and yell, 'It's the Seagull!' The guy got so pissed that he ended up quitting. He works at Market Basket now, in the seafood section. Can you believe that shit? The Seagull sells fish?"

"You can't write this," I say and my phone buzzes. A different guy. Bingo. "I can grab a gram but I have to meet the dude at the Mobil station, two blocks away, and it's pouring."

"I don't mind getting wet," Toby said.

"I'll drive you." Like a ninja, The Seagull approached from behind, without us noticing. "I'm going to the Mobil for cigarettes."

"Jimmy, you're my hero," Toby said.

"Seagull," he said. "Call me The Seagull."

Burrough's Ghosts

Another week stretched like a hamstring. I'm waiting in the Rite Aid parking lot for the Dealer's black car.

At one time, my ex-wife would wait for me in our home, on our couch, with a bowl of popcorn. She would want to binge-watch a television series, to snuggle beside me dropping a single kernel of popcorn in her mouth, one at a time.

At one time, we went on proper dates, found a babysitter for the twins, and tried to pretend we were the people we were when we fell in love, when the resentment and bitterness wasn't as real as a pinch. And she waits, knowing that I'm lost, drifting through the bad streets with the ghosts of old junkies, all of whom resembled William S. Burroughs, bone-thin with their dentures in. Blue veins bulging like crowded turnpikes. But my ex-wife could only wait so long; her patience had a shelf life.

Me and the Ghosts of Burroughs, tonight we're trying to cop, huddled around the Rite-Aid dumpster and blowing in our hands, waiting for the black car.

"I'm coming," I howl into the stupid cold of February—or maybe it's March—hoping she'll hear me. "I need you," I say as the Ghosts of Burroughs blow away, scatter like scraps of paper, and the black car pulls up, the window rolling down.

"We have your ex-wife in the trunk," the Dealer says. "Forty bucks."

I reach into my wallet and out come my teeth.

The Bubblegum Love Song

We were parked in a lot, facing Lake Massabesic. The black water rippled onto the thin shore as a half-moon hung like a broken tooth on the horizon, above the shadowy hills, those toothless and diseased gums in the distance. Zach and Tina had booted some new shit in the backseat while Tom and I smoked it in the front. It was the China White, meaning Fentanyl. I had lifted off and didn't see Zach, who had gotten out of rehab that morning, go down. I didn't see him seize. When I turned around, he was as limp as a soaked towel with his head in Tina's lap. The needle and the spoon, on the floorboard, glinted in the moonlight.

"Wake up, baby. Wake up," Tina said in the carved-out voice of a dope queen.

"He's fucking overdosing," Tom yelled over his shoulder.

"He's fine," Tina said as calm as a yield sign. "This happens all the time."

"We need to get him to the hospital," Tom said, turning over the engine. "I'm not going to let him die in my car."

Tina continued to slap Zach's face, light rhythmic taps like she was keeping the beat to a bubblegum love song. My ex-wife keeps saying "You're going to get yourself in real trouble someday doing that shit."

"I'm taking him to the hospital," Tom said.

"Don't," Tina snapped. "Drop us off at my mother's place. This happens all of the time. He's fine."

"He's fucking blue," I said although I wasn't sure if he was blue.

Tom asked Tina where her mother lived, and despite the fact that we passed the hospital on the way, Tina insisted that Tom take them to her mother's place where she said there was Narcan, if necessary. Before we arrived, Zach came to. He was still out of it but breathing. Tina kept Zach upright as they walked to the front door of a dingy duplex, Zach hanging like a smashed hinge from her shoulder.

Zach returned to rehab the next day, and while he was gone, Tina fucked Tom. Tina and Tom started booting together then they moved into

Tina's mother's place, and then Toby and I didn't see much of Tom anymore.

Toby and I hang out in a new bar, a private drinking club, where a guy in a cowboy hat and a black leather vest sells us beans when the Dealer doesn't answer his texts. Some days, we'll buy from both of them, stock up. And some days, we wait. Some days, we spend the whole day waiting for something to happen.

I'll Be Home

Waiting for the Bruise

I'm stoned, too stoned, so stoned that I'm worried that I'm going to forget how to breathe. Mike jams the glass bong in my face. "Hit it, babe," he says.

I push it away.

Mike kisses my ear, nuzzling my neck with his facial scruff.

"Stop," I say in a voice so tiny it could've come from a doll. When Mike wants me to do something, I seldom raise a fuss. He's eight years older and an Iraq War hero and muscular enough to pose on the cover of a fitness magazine.

When I look across the room, Jayce, Mike's roommate who recently got out of jail, is staring at me, licking his lips.

I focus my attention on the blue carpet that reminds me of a sick woman. It reminds me of my mom. Right now, more than anything, I want to be in my bed at Mom and Wayne's house, under my down comforter, listening to Kenny Chesney.

Mike places his hand, a vise grip, on my thigh and he squeezes it hard enough to leave a bruise. "Have another beer," he says over the rap music and shoves a Bud Light into my hand. Then he stands up and walks into the kitchen.

As soon as he leaves the room, his roommate's stare burns me, like his eyes are heat lamps. He cocks his head to the side and tries looking up my skirt. "You're fucking hot," he says.

Terrified, I swallow a sip of beer. To avoid eye contact, I stare at my cell phone and check my messages. I have a text from Mom asking where I was followed by a string of worried emojis.

Mike comes back from the kitchen and sits down beside me and places his hand on my thigh, snaking it up my skirt. I try to move it, but his fingers are too strong. I spring from the couch. "Stop it!"

Mike sighs, shaking his head, his chin down. "Why don't you call Mommy and have her bring you home? It doesn't seem like you feel like partying."

"I do, but let's go in your room," I whisper to Mike.

"Let's do a tequila shot," he says.

For a second time, Mike leaves the room, and for a second time, Jayce tries looking up my skirt as I stare at that shabby blue carpet. Stoned and drunk and scared, I can't move or speak.

"I want to lick your pussy," Jayce says.

"Stop," I say and swallow hard. I consider running from the apartment, but it's in a bad section of Manchester.

Mike comes back with three shot glasses and a bottle of Patrón. He fills the glasses and passes one of them to Jayce and another to me. While Mike and Jayce slam theirs back, I plug my nose, as if I'm about to dive into murky water, and pour the shot down my throat, coughing and gagging as the tequila drops like a hot knife in my belly.

Mike leans over and licks my neck. "You're so fucking beautiful."

"Let's go to your room."

"I have a better idea." He cups my boob. "Why don't we do it here and let Jayce record it on my phone. I want you to see how sexy you look when I'm fucking you."

I turn my head from Mike's hot liquor breath. The pot and the alcohol have scrambled my sense of balance. "I feel sick," I say to the sick blue carpet.

Mike shrugs. "If you're sick, you can call for a ride home. I'm sure we can find some girls who want to party."

So I pour another shot and choke it down. My joints turned to liquid and my head drops on Mike's lap, my blond hair landing like a parachute. I reach for his zipper, and the phone camera flashes on.

Nathan Graziano

My Real Hair

Any time you tell a real story, if the story contains a lie — even a lie through an omission — that lie will stick out like a bad wig.

So this is my real hair.

We were shopping for a coffeemaker. Like many alcoholics, my husband Mark was substituting black coffee for vodka-sodas and wanted a better coffeemaker, his reward to himself for a month of sobriety. At that point, he was white-knuckling his way through it, trying to fix his life after his first DWI. But he wouldn't go to meetings. He thought they were cultish.

"Do you think we need an espresso machine?" Mark was crouched down, squinting at a box on the bottom shelf.

"You don't drink espresso."

"I might."

Then someone tapped my shoulder, startling me. I spun around to find a tall black man, fit and fashionably dressed, looking at me with his eyebrows raised. "Lisa?"

"Sean?"

"Goddamn, I thought it was you. You look good. Real good."

When I get nervous or flirty or both, I have a habit of twirling my hair. "You, too," I said, a strand of hair spun around my ring finger.

Sean grinned and nodded and grinned. "You still got it."

Mark stood up, cradling the coffeemaker box in both arms like a newborn. He stared up at Sean as if he were watching a man on the edge of a building, wishing for him to jump. "I'm Mark," he said, a drop of sweat trickling down his pale cheek, over the dark stubble.

"How stupid," I said. "Sean, this is Mark. My husband."

"Good to meet you," Sean said, as his eyes scanned my chest.

As the other customers pushed carts and shouted prices to their significant others across the aisles, the three of us stood like we were carved from wood.

"It was good seeing you," I said to Sean. "We need to get going."

Sean grinned and nodded and grinned. "Take care." He gave me an once-over, top to bottom, then turned and walked away.

While holding a coffee maker that he hated as much as his sobriety, Mark waited for me, looking like a little boy lost in the store. I hugged him and pecked his cheek. "I dated him in college."

"You never told me you dated a black guy."

"Does it matter?"

"Did you fuck him?"

"That's racist as hell, Mark. Would you ask if he was white?"

"Yeah, probably."

"We went on a few dates," I said.

But that wasn't the whole story: it was a bad wig. The truth was that Sean was a friend of a friend in college who I slept with one night after going home with him from a bar. At the time, I had broken up with my boyfriend, who was sleeping with a TA from one of his literature classes. Sean was meant to be a one-night stand, a rebound, but we hooked up a couple of other times, late-night, when we'd see each other downtown. It's taken me awhile to admit this, but I slept with him not only to get back at my ex but to find out what it would be like to sleep with a black man. I wanted to know if the stories and stereotypes were true. In Sean's case, they were.

Mark placed the coffeemaker back on the bottom shelf.

"I thought you wanted to buy that as a present for yourself," I said.

"I changed my mind. Let's get out of here."

That night, Mark went to a bar and didn't come home. Sean sent me a "friend" request on Facebook, and I accepted.

Sasquatch

The parking lot was packed like a box of bullets. Dad and I found a spot in the back row, beneath a floodlight, and Dad cut the engine.

"Let's fuck this punk up," he said, his voice watery. A large man—almost six-nine and three hundred pounds—it takes a lot of booze to faze Dad but he had been drinking Southern Comfort since he got home from work, before I told him about the video of my step-sister on the internet, the one that had been shared throughout our high school.

A few parking spaces down from us, a popular couple from school got out of a blue sedan. When I looked over, the guy, some preppy jock-asshole named Bryce, snapped my picture with his phone. "I got a picture of the Sasquatch," he said and laughed as his girlfriend looked the other way, covering her face.

Maybe the sips of Southern Comfort I took earlier hit me harder than I realized because I slung my middle finger at the bastard and snarled like Dad when Dad snarls. And wouldn't you know it—the Bryce-asshole put the phone in his pocket, took his girlfriend's hand and walked toward the entrance to the theater.

"What was that about?" Dad asked.

"Some kid from school."

The line to buy the tickets wrapped around the side of the building. As we walked past the line, a couple of guys yelled out, "Sasquatch!" and snapped pictures with their phones.

I snarled as a white flame burned behind my eyes and I balled my fists.

When we got in the lobby, Dad stopped me. "What were those guys calling you?"

"Sasquatch, Dad. They call me Sasquatch because I'm a big hairy freak."

"Why do you put up with it?"

I shrugged. When Dad looked at me, it was as if my skin was made of glass and he could see through me into the hollowness where my guts should've been. For the first time, it was as if he understood that he had failed to raise me to be a man, that his son was something less than.

Then Dad clamped me on the shoulder. "I'm not sure if you know this, D.J., but you could wipe the shit off your shoes with any of those guys. Crack one skull and the rest will back off."

"I know, Dad. I know."

"There's the motherfucker." Dad pointed at a muscular guy with short black hair, heavily gelled and spiked, and a tribal band tattoo on his left bicep that I recognized from the video he posted on that amateur porn site. The guy was collecting ticket stubs. Dad pushed through the crowd as I followed him. Cordoned off by a purple velvet rope, Dad positioned himself in front of him, dwarfing him by at least a foot. Dad stared down at him like a boxer receiving instructions, breathing through his nostrils.

The guy, Jenny's boyfriend — his name is Mike, a war veteran who served in Iraq — watched Dad as if Dad were a small bird flapping its wings. "Back off, big fella," he said.

"You don't know who I am, do you?" Dad snarled.

"I know who you are, and I said back off, motherfucker."

As murmurs caught fire in the lobby, everyone's attention shifted toward Dad and the guy. That's when something started to grind inside me. My legs shook. The white flame pounded behind my eyes.

"Is there a problem?" The guy asked Dad in a flat, steady voice.

"Yeah," said Dad, bumping him with his chest, "there's a big fucking problem."

Dad pulled back and swung at his head but the boyfriend ducked, and before anyone could blink, he had Dad's arm bent behind his back, ready to snap it. Dad screamed.

The scream was the last thing I remember.

When the cops pulled me off him, my fists and forearms were covered in his blood. The guy who posted the video of my stepsister lay like a sack of sand on the ground, his spine snapped. I remember a lot of screaming and shouting. As I was being wrestled to my stomach and the cold cuffs were slapped on my wrists, I looked for Dad, but couldn't find him.

"What the hell got into Sasquatch?" I heard someone say. And someone else said, "I think he killed that fucking guy." Then another voice said, "You had to see that coming."

I closed my eyes and made myself real still, careful not to move, disappearing before anyone could see me and snap another picture.

The Man Who Is Fucking My Wife

The man who is fucking my wife is a cowboy —
not a cowboy in the Top Forty country music
sense, but a horseback, dust-and-grit-between-
his-teeth cowboy. He's strong-jawed and quiet,
capable of answering complex questions with a
brusque nod, or a quick grin—never anything
polysyllabic. He shaves on Tuesday mornings and
Saturday evenings before he hits the town, and he
has a way of making Old Spice smell nostalgic.
The sun has given his skin a tight, leathered
look, and when he smiles—which isn't often—it
stretches his face like a belt.

The man who is fucking my wife has a chest
like John Wayne and can don a duster like Clint
Eastwood. He votes a straight Republican ticket
and makes no apologies. He views economic issues
as things that people need to fix for themselves and

social issues as frivolous, although he'd never use that word. He speaks using conservative clichés: "There's no such thing as a free ride" or "You can't help someone who won't help themselves." Yet he has a way a making a bleeding heart woman, like my wife, believe things were really better when we all rode horses.

The man who is fucking my wife is the American cowboy paradigm, who wears the white hat in spaghetti Westerns; whose top lip never shivers after a shot of rot-gut; who keeps a toothpick in the corner of his mouth and flips it with his tongue; who expects a full ten minutes of head before intercourse.

The man who is fucking my wife has a gargantuan cock, a cock that coils and impresses a distinctive bulge when he wears tight, faded blue jeans. He's no enigma.

When my wife unzips his fly and reaches into his briefs, her eyes widen and she wets her lips. She looks the cowboy in the eyes and says, "My, my."

Moon Walk

When Lisa and I split, she took the house, most of the furniture, and our one respectable car. Yet she cheated on me. Go figure. I was renting a cheap one-bedroom place in a bad part of the city and had spiraled into a stormy bender. One day melted into the next, a week melted into the next interminable week, all of it boiling in a cracked caldron of self-loath.

I was three weeks deep into my new bender and pretty tight the night Jackson called. It was the first time I'd heard from him in five years, and he called to tell me his plane would be arriving in Manchester-Boston Regional Airport at ten-fifteen p.m. Jackson—a beefy guy whose real name was Brian Unger—gave birth to the nickname one night when he did an improbably perfect moon walk across some filthy kitchen tiles while shit-faced at a frat party. When Jackson called me from O'Hare in Chicago, he said that he and his wife Stacey were on the skids, and that's all he said. I wrote the flight number on the back of a phone bill then drove—with a suspended license after a second DWI—heavy-lidded and sweaty, to the airport in my dented Honda Accord with a Styrofoam cooler of cold Coors Light in the backseat.

While waiting for Jackson at the gate, I passed the time eying a pretty young girl in a yellow sundress who was chewing her nails to the cuticles. After blowing into my hand and smelling my breath—yes, it reeked of beer—I began to inch closer. Her smooth golden legs spilled from the hem of her dress like two cold drinks, cold drinks capable of washing down the acrid taste Lisa left on the back of my tongue, a taste I couldn't seem to swallow. Dressed in a sweaty white t-shirt, cargo shorts and sandals, I was dressed for Jackson, not a pretty young girl in a yellow sundress. She was out of my league, inconceivable to me.

"Are you waiting for someone?" I asked the pretty young girl in the yellow dress. I hadn't spoken socially to a woman since Lisa and I split, and only now does it occur to me how ridiculous the question was.

She gave me the once-over then rolled her eyes. "I'm waiting for my boyfriend."

"Have you been together long?"

"We met on the internet."

"Be careful," I said. "Make sure he's not a serial killer."

"Thank you for your concern."

A sweet Southern voice announced the arrival of the flight from O'Hare, and I stepped back from the pretty young girl in the yellow sundress and waited for Jackson. One of the first guys out of the gate was the boyfriend, and I watched the young girl's face stiffen into a fixed smile of a jack-o-lantern, one golden leg trembling.

Jackson was the last person out of the tunnel, drunk and disheveled. We shook hands and patted each other on the back. "Mark, my friend, I'm wearing another man's underwear," Jackson said.

"Jackson, what the fuck?"

"They're these red marble-bag man-panties, but I didn't have anything clean, so I put them on. Stacey must be humping a male stripper. Normal guys don't wear man-panties."

"How do they feel?" I watched as the pretty young girl in a yellow sundress planted a dry kiss on the lips of the serial killer.

"Tight, man," Jackson said. "Really tight."

A Long Way from New Hampshire

A couple of creeps come out of the gas station carrying six-packs and staring at me the way older men sometimes stare at me. I'm standing in front of the propane tanks, waiting for Aaron and his cousin to get back from wherever they went to buy weed. We're in Brownsville, Tennessee, a long way from New Hampshire, and I'm unsafe. Aaron grew up here, but he's gone and these creeps look like the types of rednecks who might throw a canvas sack over my head and drive me out to the hills.

Mom used to say to me, "Jenny, there are some men who don't understand 'no.' When you meet one, run."

It's obvious what these creeps are thinking, but Mom is a thousand miles away and dying a slow death. Now I'm fending for myself. Lost, a long way from New Hampshire.

I'm hoping these creeps will just take a long look and keep walking, but they stop in front of me. The taller of the two creeps, a guy with a lazy eye that makes him creepier, holds out a Budweiser can. "Want a beer, honey?" he asks with this syrupy Southern accent.

"No thanks. I'm waiting for someone."

"Ain't you the sweetest little Yankee-girl," says the tall creep. He winks at me. "I'm Jake, and this here is Keith but we call him Mutt. We got some weed in the truck."

"My boyfriend will be back any minute," I say and look the other way.

"He ain't here now," Jake says then laughs. "We can drive around a little, get a good buzz on, and have you back in ten minutes, Yankee girl."

"No thanks." My skin is prickling. Not again, I think. I want to scream but I can't get enough air in my lungs. I should run into the store but my legs are shaking. Not again.

"I'm not sure where you're from, baby," Jake says, hissing in my ear, his breath heavy with beer. "I reckon it's some big Yankee city. But around these parts, sweet tits, if you hang out in front of stores wearing shorts like those with those big ole' titties hanging out of your shirt, some guys are gonna get the wrong idea."

The other guy, Mutt, spits in the dirt. "Cocktease."

They walk to their pick-up truck as my heart stammers, waiting. Then they jump in and rev the engine. I exhale. While driving past me, Mutt sticks his head out the passenger window. "Fuckin' Yankee cunt!"

The back tires spin and the truck peels out of the parking lot.

Dark clouds scurry across the sky and a breeze whips through my hair, which I've dyed jet-black. A raindrop falls on my cheek, and another on my forearm, and then another on my nose. Mom, I want to come home.

Nathan Graziano

Almost Christmas

Jackson told me over the telephone that this new girl he'd been dating liked to be choked and slapped while getting fucked.

I said, "Jackson, this isn't going to end well."

The beer bottles were lined up, two finger-lengths apart, on the table in front of me, one plugged with wet cigarette butts. I had the phone book spread open and the number for Alcoholics Anonymous underlined in pencil. I told myself I was going to find a meeting as soon as I got off the phone with Jackson. The next morning, I was heading to jail—doing ten days in county after my second DWI. Something like a clenched fist had been floating in the center of my chest for weeks, a hardened pit of fear. I'd never been to jail and never imagined I would. I'm soft. And somewhere, at that very moment, my ex-wife was probably fucking her black boyfriend, straddling him in the same bed where we once slept. And somewhere, Jackson's first wife was probably fucking this cop she'd been seeing, while Jackson was talking to me about his new girl, a divorcee who worked at the Target in Saginaw and liked to be roughed up. And somewhere, even farther away, there was this vague recollection, the dimmest of the dim stars, that all of this, at one time, used to be fun.

A beer popped on the other end of the line. "The other morning, when I was coming out of the shower," Jackson paused and sipped and burped. "And Mark, I'm not shitting you, my friend. Cindy was standing in front of my bedroom mirror in her bra and panties, talking to herself in a baby voice. Then she turned to me and asked, in this baby-voice, if I'd choke her."

"Did you?"

"I couldn't."

It was almost Christmas, and the convenience store across the street had recently put a single plastic candle behind the bars in the front window. It hummed to me. "Jackson, you're a good man."

"No, I'm not," he said, and kept drinking.

Nathan Graziano

Nathan Graziano lives in Manchester, New Hampshire. His recent books include *Hangover Breakfasts* (Bottle of Smoke Press, 2012), *Sort Some Sort of Ugly* (Marginalia Publishing, 2013), and *My Next Bad Decision* (Artistically Declined Press, 2014). He writes a baseball column for *Dirty Water Sports* in Boston. For more information, visit his website:

www.nathangraziano.com

Redneck Press is the chapbook-publishing arm of Fried Chicken and Coffee, a blogazine of on-off rants, rural, working class and Appalachian concerns, with occasional crime fiction.

www.friedchickenandcoffee.com